WINNERS

WINNERS

First published by Authors Tree Publishing

Editing & Cover Design: Authors Tree Publishing

India: INR ₹195/-

ISBN: 978-93-47208-23-2

9 789347 208232

Authors Tree Publishing
Bilaspur, Chhattisgarh
Pin: 495001
Call: +91 9109886656
www.authorstree.com
First Edition. 2026
Printed in India

WINNERS

by
NIRAV PARIKH

Preface

Our world has become a very difficult place to survive. Life is not as simple and happy as it used to be in past. With every passing day, we observe the rapid changes around us, which create a challenging environment that frequently brings negativity into our lives. People are frustrated, depressed and demotivated. Everything feels sad.

So, what makes one happy? The most exciting feeling of life. The feeling of winning. You feel like an achiever. Someone better than others, someone who can not only survive but also progress, someone who can set a benchmark. When you win, you start believing in yourself, you become more confident and you celebrate your victory with everyone. You are a winner. Such winners are the central characters of all the short stories I have written in this book.

Even though Winners is a complete work of fiction, it is inspired by real-life people I met and challenging situations I faced in my life, which motivated me to move forward and win. I wanted to share these stories with everyone, so I wrote this book.

Thank you for picking up my book from the lot. I hope Winners creates a positive impact on your life as we hope for a better tomorrow.

Just have a look how high is the tide
The time has come for most awaited ride
Challenging is the task, hiding behind the mask
At every step, a new question someone will ask
Ability will be tested during each phase
Everyone wants to be ahead in the race
Losing is painful can break you apart
Your past will firmly say not to restart
Don't be depressed, don't lose hope
Life offers a huge amount of scope
Keep moving forward, changing the sail
Try again and again, even if you fail
Because when many failures are piled on
In this world, WINNERS are born...

Contents

The Birthday Gift

Nisarg Shah is a perfect man. He is smart, handsome, intelligent, rich, well mannered, disciplined and successful. An all-in-one package. At 29, Nisarg is India's youngest self-made billionaire. Within a span of 5 years, his tech startup has made remarkable profits, won numerous awards and has been named the most employee-friendly company to work for. This is a result of Nisarg's passion to achieve in life. From high profile corporate events to elite parties, Nisarg Shah captures everyone's attention wherever he goes. He is a gem of a person. All men want to be like him and all women want to be with him.

Today is a special day. It's her birthday. The one whom Nisarg loves the most in this world. She is the most important person in his life. Nothing matters to him more than her. So, after winding up all his important work and meetings in the first half of the day, Nisarg left his office to buy a birthday gift for his special one.

As he reached the largest gift store in the city, Nisarg was warmly greeted by Rahul, the store owner, as he was one of his oldest customers.

Rahul's gift store is located inside a huge cubicle spanning the entire floor of a mega mall and it is full of gifts divided into various categories such as soft toys, paintings, souvenirs, handicrafts, hangouts and much more. There were also unique options for customising gifts. While so many options always make things confusing for the buyer, Nisarg decided to take help from Rahul.

"This time I need something really special and unique as a birthday gift for her," said Nisarg.

"Of course, sir, I will show you our exclusive and customised collection," replied Rahul.

"I'm eager to see your collection. But remember, the birthday gift should be extremely unique," said Nisarg.

"Definitely, sir," replied Rahul.

Rahul placed 12 of the most unique items from his gift catalogue, which included never seen before handcrafted ornaments, accessories with beautiful embroidery and some of the most innovatively designed products, such as scarves, bracelets, leather bags, etc., created for elegant women. But none of these impressed Nisarg.

Rahul further recommended some high end luxury gifts. Nisarg thought of buying one of them but later rejected his idea, as such gifts did not serve his purpose.

Nisarg decided to explore the gift store on his own. After browsing through many sections, all of a sudden he spotted a globe made of glass kept on a display shelf. Nisarg picked up the globe and gave it a spin. He enjoyed the view of the entire world, from continents to oceans, displayed on the crystal clear glass. It reminded him of something. Nisarg decided to buy it as a birthday gift.

“I really like this glass globe. Kindly pack this one for me,” said Nisarg.

“Sir, she won't like this. I suggest not buying this one. We have much better products in our gift catalogue,” replied Rahul.

“It's all right. This is my final choice,” said Nisarg.

“As you wish, sir,” said Rahul.

After purchasing the birthday gift, Nisarg left the gift store to meet her. He believed that birthday is the most important day in the annual calendar, as it celebrates the birth of a person in this world and how life brings unexpected surprises with growing age. A birthday is all about celebrating life and looking forward to many more special moments in the years to come.

As Nisarg was driving, his heart was filled with happiness and excitement, waiting to see her reaction after receiving her birthday gift.

After beating the hectic traffic, Nisarg finally reached his destination. As the sun was about to set, she was sitting on a swing in the lawn outside her home, completely lost in the book she was reading. Nisarg quickly ran from behind and covered her eyes with his hands. She immediately recognised him because of his tender touch. Nisarg then took her to a scheduled spot where he had placed the birthday gift. Slowly, he took his hands off her eyes. As she opened her eyes, she saw a glass globe placed on the ground next to her feet.

"As promised to you a long time ago, today I place the entire world under your feet. In my life, you are the perfect fit and this big world is your small gift. Happy Birthday, Mom!" said Nisarg.

"Thank you, Nisarg. This is stunning," replied his mother, who was completely surprised by her son.

"After Dad expired at an early stage of my life, you raised me as a single parent. You worked as a banker and as a mother at the same time, balancing your professional and personal life. From preparing my tiffin box to financing my higher studies, you gave me everything I needed even before I requested it. You spent sleepless nights sitting next to me when I was unwell. You struggled in your present for my better future. You fulfilled all my wishes by sacrificing yours. Today, whatever I am is because of your efforts. You have always been an inspiration to me. Thank you for everything, Mom," said Nisarg.

“This glass globe will always be a memorable birthday gift for me, but the best gift of my life is you, Nisarg. The day I gave birth to you was the happiest day of my life. And now my son has become so big that he puts the entire world under my feet,” said his mother with tears in her eyes.

She gave Nisarg a tight hug. It felt like the whole world had come to a halt for a while. Then both of them went to cut the birthday cake and celebrate the special day, making it a memory to cherish forever. Nothing matters more to a mother than her child and for every child, his mother remains the most valuable person in his life.

LEVEL 7

Level 7 is the most downloaded mobile game on all app stores. Within a few days after its release, the game became an instant hit among mobile gamers. Known for its addictive play format, Level 7 also promises to be a highly engaging, entertaining and educational game. It recently received the 'Best Mobile Game of the Year' award from the Google Play. Tech Zone magazine reporter Nishika Kaur interviews its creator, Manan Mehta, on his Level 7 journey so far.

Nishika: From maximum downloads to winning awards, Level 7 has emerged as a winner in all ways. Did you expect this while creating the game?

Manan: Of course not. I just wanted to create something that is enjoyable and useful to everyone. If you want to create something extraordinary, you can't keep success in mind while creating it because it will restrict your ability to constantly experiment and try out new things.

Nishika: Tell us more about Level 7.

Manan: Level 7 is named after the 7 difficulty levels of the game. Each level has multiple challenges that the gamer has to complete to qualify for the next level. As the gamer makes progress, the challenges become more difficult and tricky. A gamer will be tested on various parameters like logic, planning, execution, judgment, etc. The gamer who clears the final Level 7 with the maximum score is the ultimate winner and his name gets displayed on the high score board, which becomes a score to beat for other gamers. The best gamers of the year are given a place in the 'Level 7 Hall of Fame'.

Nishika: Why do you think Level 7 became an instant hit among gamers?

Manan: Its addictive gameplay. A gamer gets a chance to do interesting things as part of the game challenges. From managing an amusement park to creating a fantasy cricket team, from hunting hidden artifacts in a 3D maze to customising a bicycle, the game is a combination of various factors rolled into one. At regular intervals, real-world trivia related to the challenge is shared with gamers. A quiz is conducted based on trivia on our Facebook page and winners are rewarded with cool Level 7 merchandise. So, Level 7 is engaging, entertaining, educational and rewarding. Gamers nationwide enjoy this all-in-one package and also recommend Level 7 to others.

Nishika: What was the biggest challenge you came across while creating Level 7 and how did you overcome it?

Manan: Project timeline. While we had our team of experts from every field, completing and launching the game on time was our biggest challenge. As the launch date was already planned and announced, there were many things that were getting delayed as per our product roadmap. This delay would result in postponing the launch, which we could not afford at any cost. So, we had a few meetings and made certain changes in our plan, like focusing more on quality rather than quantity. We removed certain sections that did not make much difference and were time consuming. We decided to focus on the major areas of Level 7 like content, graphics and gameplay. The features that did not perform well during the game testing phase were not rectified but removed. These features will later be available in the updated version of Level 7 after its launch.

Nishika: Industry experts say Level 7 could have been a much bigger success if you had created it as a Virtual Reality (VR) game. Do you agree?

Manan: Yes. There is no doubt about the fact that Virtual Reality is the future of gaming. In the case of Level 7 as a VR game, its production cost would have been much higher and VR gear is expensive, which would have resulted in attracting a limited number of gamers. As a mobile game, Level 7 has appealed to a much larger base since everyone owns a smartphone and the game is completely free for all.

Nishika: If Level 7 is a free game, how do you generate revenue from it?

Manan: Level 7 was never made with the intention to earn money. A past incident from my life resulted in its creation. Of course, there is a cost involved in creating a game that needs to be recovered. For that, we came up with bonus levels. These bonus levels can be accessed by paying a subscription fee. We are also planning to add more bonus levels in the future. Level 7 also has in-app purchases, branded content, sponsorships and event tie-ups for game monetisation. We have also received contracts from the country's leading educational institutions for creating games similar to Level 7, which has opened doors for a B2B revenue model.

Nishika: Would you like to share the incident that resulted in the creation of Level 7?

Manan: Of course! When I was an engineering student, I used to go for an evening walk in the park close to my home. I noticed a 12-year-old boy who used to come to the park and sit on the bench holding a bat and a ball in his hands. He used to do this every day. Out of growing curiosity, one day I approached him and asked him why he didn't play. He told me he was new to the city, as his father had recently got a job transfer. He did not have any friends in the locality, as none of them belonged to his age group.

Every day he came to the park hoping he would find someone with whom he could play cricket. I saw sadness, loneliness and depression on the boy's face. In such situations, these aspects grow with time, which results in addiction to smoking, drugs and even suicide cases due to mental depression. I never wanted something like that to happen to him. Hence, I decided to play with him. I remember the smile on that boy's face when he was batting for the first time we played. I wanted to see that smile on the face of every unhappy person in the world.

As time passed, technology made huge progress and I discovered that mobile gaming can be the solution to growing sadness, loneliness and depression in this world, as everyone now owns a smartphone and the option to play solo is easily available. That was when I decided to create Level 7. Since many games were known for their negative features like violence and adverse effects on the human brain, we assembled a team of psychologists, art directors, tech geeks and educational experts and created Level 7 with detailed research and insights from everyone. A game all set to share valuable knowledge in a fun-filled format and bring a smile to every lonely and depressed face. Today, when I see that smile on the faces of all Level 7 gamers, I feel satisfied that I have achieved my goal.

Nishika: What are your future plans?

Manan: Level 7 is just the beginning. My mission is to eradicate loneliness and depression through gaming while adding a fun learning factor to it. I still have a long way to go. We are planning to create sequel versions of the Level 7 game and also launch new games based on the feedback and suggestions we have received from gamers and industry experts. Right now, I will take a step back, understand what inspires me and match that with what the world needs. After a short break, I will be back with something much more exciting and never experienced before by anyone.

Nishika: This sounds really cool. Wishing you the best for your upcoming projects.

Manan: Thanks a lot, Nishika. It was a wonderful experience interacting with you.

Technology has been criticised by many for its negative impact on humans, but there are people like Manan Mehta who have a vision for using technology to bring happiness and positivity with a fun-filled approach for sharing knowledge with everyone. By focusing on invention and innovation, one can utilise technology to a large extent for creating a better tomorrow.

Together Forever

In the beginning, married life seems like a joyride. Husband and wife spend a lot of time together, interacting about their life experiences, weekend outings, vacation trips and finding joy in doing simple things like shopping in a supermarket or decorating the home during the festive season. But with passing time, this happiness begins to fade. Work becomes a priority over personal life, leading to regular fights at home, silent and lonely weekends and a growing feeling of hatred towards each other.

Raj and Radhika have been married for 2 years and like every married couple, with passing time, their relationship is going through a rough phase. Constantly changing priorities based on unexpected situations, balancing personal and professional life and disagreements due to differences in opinion are some of the key factors behind the growing distance between them. It was a Friday evening and Raj had just entered his home only to find out that Radhika had arrived before him.

"Radhika, if you were coming early today, you should have informed me," said Raj.

"Why? So that you can assign me household tasks?" replied an irritated Radhika.

"What is wrong with that? I perform my part of the household duties. This is our home," said Raj.

"I left my parents, family and past life, everything behind for this home," screamed Radhika.

"I have made many more sacrifices than you have. From destroying my personal wish list to working non-stop for our better future. After we got married, there was nothing about me; everything was about us. You always had a one-sided approach towards life. You only think about yourself. Your choices, your likes, your way of living. There is no point in explaining to you. Just go to hell," shouted Raj.

"Hell would have been a better option than marrying you," replied Radhika.

An angry and irritated Raj went to the bedroom and banged the door so hard that it could permanently damage a person's hearing ability. Radhika went to the other bedroom as she hated the feeling of sharing a bed with her husband and wanted to sleep alone. The night passed in complete silence.

As Saturday being a holiday, both Raj and Radhika were at home. Both of them behaved like strangers, completely ignoring each other's presence. In the evening, Raj wanted to spend some time away from the toxic and suffocating atmosphere at home, so he decided to visit Xpress Café for a refreshing experience. Radhika was also happy being alone at home.

At Xpress Café…

"Don't worry, Raj, everything will be fine," said Ishita as she gently placed her hand on his wrist. "Even I used to think like that in the beginning, Ishita, but with every passing day, things are getting worse," said Raj.

Raj and Ishita met each other when they were working for the same company. At that point in time, Raj was not married. Both of them used to spend a lot of time together and Ishita understood Raj very well. Even after Ishita left the company to start her own PR agency, she and Raj remained good friends. A few years later, Raj got married to Radhika, while Ishita is still single due to her work commitments. Raj and Ishita used to meet occasionally at Xpress Café near her office.

"I think you both should take a break from work and travel to some calm destination," suggested Ishita.
"That will just make things worse between us. Even a weekend is like punishment and you are suggesting a vacation? No way," replied Raj.

"You both should discuss this situation with your parents and in-laws. They have better life experience and will definitely provide a suitable solution," suggested Ishita.

"There is no chance of doing that. Managing a family was a much easier task for them as survival and growth were not a challenge during those days. Now times have changed, the way of living has changed and their solutions won't work for the current situation. I thought about every possible option, but nothing seems to work out. Every day I feel suffocated at home and I have started spending more time in the office these days," replied Raj.

"Raj, if it is so difficult, then you should not continue with this relationship. You should seriously consider filing for a divorce. Sometimes in life, it is better to let things go, after which you can make a fresh start," said Ishita.

Raj gave it a thought and then smiled at Ishita. She got a bit confused by his reaction.

"Ishita, your suggestion is really worth considering, but that is never going to happen. When I married Radhika, I already knew life would never be the same. Two unknown people born and brought up in different surroundings are going to start a new life together. It will never be that easy. Life will be full of problems and running away is not an option because tomorrow a new problem will arise. At the time of our marriage, both of us knew we were made for each other and decided that no matter what happens, we will always be together forever. Every married couple should understand that if their relationship is going through a rough phase, that does not mean the husband is bad or the wife is bad; it is the situation that is bad and both of them need to overcome it together," explained Raj.

"Hmmm… I really like your approach, Raj, but remember, if you need any kind of help or want to share something, you always have me as a friend," replied Ishita.

"Thanks, Ishita. Now I must leave. I have a situation to handle at home," said Raj.

On his way, Raj decided that he would try to explain their family situation to Radhika and also understand what Radhika thinks about it. There is always hope for a better tomorrow.

As Raj entered his home, he saw a teddy bear with 'I am sorry' card attached to it placed on the sofa. As Raj picked it up for a closer look, Radhika rushed towards Raj and gave him a tight hug.

"I am sorry, Raj. I just don't understand what happened to me. I should have never behaved in such a manner with the man whom I love the most," said Radhika.

"I am sorry, Radhika. I also should have controlled my temper. Don't worry, we will sort this out," replied Raj.

Marriage is a journey that both husband and wife have to travel together. It is a lifetime commitment. When a couple ties the knot and completes seven steps and vows in the presence of fire, it marks the beginning of a new chapter in life. Unexpected obstacles lie ahead and time will test them at every phase, but nothing can set them apart if they are prepared to be together forever.

Right or Wrong

Every person comes across a situation in his life where he is not able to differentiate between right and wrong. There is a constant battle going on in the mind about taking the next step and its consequences. What seems right to your mind might be wrong according to your heart and soul. Such a situation is extremely challenging and it will test your decision making ability in the most unexpected way. One such situation came in the life of adventure enthusiast trekker Chaddi.

Chandresh Divan is commonly known by his nickname ‘Chaddi', a mashup of his first name and last name and being a nature lover and trekker, he wore chaddi (half-pants) during his trips as it proved to be a highly compatible outfit during adventure activities like nature trekking, rock climbing, rappelling, rafting, river crossing and so on. Chaddi respected nature in all forms and believed that it is the best gift to mankind. He also gave equal importance to protecting the elements of nature to ensure the survival of future generations of humans. In his personal life too, Chaddi is committed to a vegetarian diet, as he is strictly against the killing of birds and animals.

Chaddi works as Editorial Head of Travelogue, a leading travel magazine that publishes hidden gems of nature from all over the world. Chaddi enjoyed his work as it matched his passion for nature. During his research to compile content for Travelogue, Chaddi used to come across many unknown places that had dense forests, waterfalls, turquoise lakes and snow-capped mountains. Collecting this information, he used to create his own itineraries and go on solo trips. Finally, the year is about to end and as usual, Chaddi has taken leave from his work for his next adventure.

On an extremely chilly winter morning, Western Ghats mountain range felt like a serene paradise. The early morning fog, cold weather and fresh air were a treat for any nature lover. Chaddi is on a hike that spanned across three mountains through a connecting trail. After trekking all day long through dense forests, waterfalls, rough terrains and dimly lit areas, Chaddi came across a nice mini waterfall where he had his lunch under a tree with an unbeatable view. Later, he continued his hike with the help of his GPS. This entire trail ends at a beautiful lake where one can see the reflection of all three mountains in it. As time passed, Chaddi realised that it would take one more day to reach the lake where the hike ends. He wondered how sometimes on GPS things appear to be close, but in reality, they are very far.

As the sun was about to set, Chaddi came across an empty spot with sufficient open space ideal for a campsite. He decided to spend the night there by setting up a makeshift tent and campfire. While having dinner, Chaddi used to think about how the day went, how such experiences made his life different from the rest of the people living in this world and above all, how being alone and disconnected helps a person rediscover himself. After an exhaustive day followed by the chilly wind of the night, sleep came quickly to Chaddi as he went in his tent and zipped it from the inside. He opened his sleeping bag, placed his head on a mini pillow and closed his eyes. The night was cold and calm.

The next day arrived with a ray of sunlight inside the tent in the early morning, but Chaddi was in deep sleep. Suddenly, he woke up because of a constantly disturbing sound. As he unzipped his tent and stepped out, he saw something he had never imagined in his dreams.

A grown-up tiger cub is in front of him with one of its rear legs trapped in a twisted loop of tree roots.

The tiger cub is constantly pushing, pulling and jumping to remove his leg from the loop but failing repeatedly. The tiger cub is frustrated and furious. Chaddi quickly understood the situation. At night, after the campfire went out, the lost tiger cub was exploring the forest to find its way back home and due to the darkness, was unable to spot the web of tree roots. As a result, one of his legs, being small, got trapped in it and the whole night the tiger cub was unable to free itself.

Now the tiger cub is in extreme pain, constantly struggling to free itself and Chaddi had two options.

Option 1: Make an attempt to free the tiger cub. He is a victim of a bad situation and desperately needs help.

Option 2: Completely ignore what is in front of his eyes, pack up and leave the campsite.

While both options seemed right to Chaddi, they also felt wrong at the same time. If Chaddi went for option 1, there is a huge risk involved, as the tiger cub might think that this was a trap set up by a human and attack Chaddi after being freed. Despite being a tiger cub, it is a grown-up one and its attack could leave Chaddi brutally wounded. It is also possible that the tiger cub could die during the tussle if Chaddi accidentally harmed him as an act of self-defence. Chaddi knew very well about the constant drop in the population of tigers and how important it is to ensure their survival.

If Chaddi went for option 2, it would be a very safe bet for him. Ignore and mind his own business. But at the same time, Chaddi, being a committed nature lover and protector, could not afford this at any cost. What would happen to the tiger cub after he left? Would the tiger cub be able to free itself? What if someone else found the tiger cub in this situation and took advantage of it? What about the family of this tiger cub, which is based somewhere in the forest? Would they come searching for him? Anything could happen.

After an in-depth mental analysis of both options, Chaddi decided to go ahead with Option 1. But before making an attempt to free the tiger cub, Chaddi needed to prepare for his defence as well. He took the extra pieces of wood that he had collected for the campfire and placed them in a linear sequence towards the escape route. He also applied an inflammable spray on them. After packing all his essentials, he began his actual mission.

First of all, Chaddi ignited the pieces of wood after entering the area where the tiger cub is trapped. As Chaddi approached step by step, on seeing him, the tiger cub tried to jump and attack as it sensed danger but was unable to cause any harm due to his leg being tied up in tree roots. Chaddi took his pillow cover and gently placed it on the tiger cub's face, blocking its vision temporarily. Then he took out his Swiss Army knife and started cutting the twisted loop. A few seconds later, he succeeded in freeing the tiger cub. Chaddi quickly ran and jumped across the fire from the point where its effect was minimal.

In the meantime, the tiger cub was able to remove the pillow cover placed on his face. As he saw fire in front of his eyes, the tiger cub decided to escape through the back route as he was completely relieved from his pain and night long struggle for freedom. Chaddi took quick steps towards the main road leading to a small village close by using his

GPS. Thanks to his 'chaddi' outfit, he was able to walk fast. He only had one thing in mind: reach the village before the fire died completely, or the tiger cub might return trailing his marks. After a few minutes, Chaddi reached the village, from where he took an alternate route guided by the villagers to the lake, which is the endpoint of his nature trail.

On the way, Chaddi thought about what if his decision of choosing option 1 had been wrong? What if the tiger cub had attacked him? What if he had harmed the tiger cub unintentionally? Even in such scenarios, his decision would have been termed right as he made an attempt to save the tiger cub. Right or wrong is not important. What matters is the end result. A happy and satisfying feeling. The tiger cub is saved, Chaddi is safe, all is well.

Dream Home

Home is where your heart lies. It is a place where you can find peace, prosperity and privacy. It is a place where you can experience the best moments of life with your family members and create great memories. It is a place where you get a feeling of self-belonging. Every person has a strong desire to buy their own dream home where everything will be as per his wish. While searching for such a dream home is a challenging and time-consuming task, some people don't give up and firmly believe that one day their dream home will be a part of their real life.

Siddharth is currently living in his father's home along with his wife Harshita and his 10-year-old son, Purav. While his father's home is huge enough for his parents, wife and son, Siddharth has always had a dream of buying his own home and living separately with Harshita and Purav as a nuclear family. He had a vision of his dream home, which included an extremely spacious drawing room, a comfortable master bedroom, a colourful kids' room, a modular kitchen with a dining table and a posh location with green surroundings. Siddharth firmly believed that such a dream home does exist in the real world and he would do whatever it takes to find and purchase it for his family.

Siddharth began his journey of house hunting by selecting his preferred location and then shortlisting a few upcoming projects in that location. Siddharth used to go house hunting every weekend. Most of the flats he saw were newly constructed ones and were designed as per the current way of living. Siddharth noticed one major negative in all newly constructed buildings, which was less carpet area, while spacious rooms were one of the major requirements of his dream home. Also, newly constructed flats had other disadvantages, such as a higher tax amount and maintenance cost, which would result in unnecessary expenses in the long run. As a result, Siddharth completely dropped the plan of buying a newly constructed flat directly from the builder.

Siddharth got in touch with a real estate agent who is an expert in the locality where he wanted to buy a flat. The agent showed him many flats, but none of them were impressive. Also, many resale flats had some strong negative features such as dirty and unhygienic surroundings, poorly maintained buildings, locations in extreme interiors, which would create travelling hassle, improper internal layout and so on. Siddharth had clearly mentioned his criteria to the real estate agent, but none of the flats shown to him had the key essentials. Siddharth also got in touch with a few other real estate agents, but his experience was the same.

Finally, Siddharth decided to search for his dream home completely on his own. He followed a two-way approach where he advertised his requirements so that sellers could contact him and he referred to the advertisements posted directly by owners who wanted to sell their flats. After a few weeks, Siddharth came across an ad of a flat on a real estate portal that had a description exactly like his dream home. He contacted the owner, Mr. Kulkarni and fixed an appointment.

Siddharth met Mr. Kulkarni and saw his flat. He was completely surprised. His dream home is in front of his eyes, exactly the way he wanted it. The internal layout, exterior lobby, plot area, location, surrounding locality, transport connectivity, everything is there as per his wish. He actually took multiple rounds of the flat, both internally and externally, with a microscopic look till he is completely satisfied. Finally, after 2 years, his search for a dream home came to an end. Siddharth requested Mr. Kulkarni for a second visit as he wanted to show the flat to his wife Harshita and son Purav.

A week later, Siddharth made a second visit to the flat along with Harshita and Purav. He had not revealed to them that the flat he had shortlisted is exactly like his dream home. He wanted them to experience the same surprise as his first visit. When Harshita and Purav saw the flat, they could not believe their eyes. While Harshita fell in love with the home at first sight, Purav refused to step out of the kids' room once he entered it. Both of them immediately requested Siddharth to buy it.

"Mr. Kulkarni, your flat meets all my key requirements. I am interested in buying your flat. You know, such perfection is hard to find these days," said Siddharth.

"That's correct. Actually, this building was a government project for employees working in a government bank. Later, the bank employees took ownership of their respective flats through an internal employee loan scheme by the bank. Hence, it is so perfect and well-maintained. I never wanted to sell my flat, but as I have retired and I am shifting back to my hometown, this flat is of no use to me. Also, by selling it, I will avoid unnecessary maintenance and repair costs, taxes, etc. This is also a highly profitable deal for you, Siddharth," said Mr. Kulkarni.

"Highly profitable deal? Am I missing out on something here?" questioned Siddharth.

"Yes. I did not reveal this to you earlier, but this entire building will be undergoing redevelopment after 2 years. The contract for redevelopment has been given to a very reputable builder. Post the redevelopment of this building, this flat will have 1 additional bedroom with an attached bathroom and many other facilities like podium parking, a kids' play area in the plot and much more. As a result, you will have more space to live comfortably in this flat and in future, if you wish to sell this flat, it will fetch you a much higher price," revealed Mr. Kulkarni.

This news came as a big shock to Siddharth. His dream home is valid only for 2 years, post which it would be permanently destroyed. Siddharth is not at all excited by the redevelopment offer as the new building, its internal layout and entire planning would be as per the builder's vision and not his dream. Siddharth informed Mr. Kulkarni that he is no longer interested in buying his flat and left the place with Harshita and Purav.

"Don't worry, Siddharth, you will definitely find your dream home. This flat itself was an indication that you are very close to your dream home," said Harshita.

"I don't think that is going to happen, Harshita. Even if I do find my dream home, there is no guarantee that it will remain exactly the way it is forever. Anything can happen. Luckily, in this case, we came to know about the future plans and cancelled the deal, but what if something similar happens after we buy our dream home?" questioned Siddharth.

Siddharth continued his search and finally purchased a flat that met the majority of his requirements. Even though this flat is not perfect like Mr. Kulkarni's flat, Siddharth, Harshita and Purav were very happy and satisfied after shifting to their new home. This deal also proved to be a highly profitable one for Siddharth as he purchased the flat at a lower price compared to Mr. Kulkarni's flat.

After living in this home for 3 years, this building also underwent redevelopment. After 4 years, the redevelopment project was completed and Siddharth got possession of his newly constructed flat. The new version, with additional benefits, is better than its previous version. What surprised Siddharth the most was that this new version of his home is the closest match to his vision of a dream home. Finally, Siddharth, Harshita and Purav moved into their new home and started living their dream.

Dream home is not the one where everything is perfect. There is always something missing, as the real world constantly keeps changing. Just imagine a place where you can discover happiness and a feeling of internal satisfaction for yourself and your family. Such a place is your dream home.

Checkmate

Chess is one such game where the sharpest minds of the world compete against each other on a small board of 64 squares. Right from the beginning, every chess player looks for an opportunity to checkmate his opponent and plans his moves accordingly. Checkmate is a game position in chess where a player's king is captured by the pieces of his opponent and there is no way for the king to escape. The player who checkmates his opponent wins the game. Checkmate is also the most preferred option by chess players to defeat their opponents because it avoids unnecessary extension of the game and a draw situation where nobody wins.

The strong desire to checkmate has resulted in fierce rivalry among chess players. One of the most popular rivalries was between Anand Iyer from India and Igor Petrov from Russia. Both of them were Grandmasters, the highest title given to chess players. Anand and Igor met each other for the first time at an under-18 international chess tournament. While it was Anand's first chess tournament outside India, Igor had played at European and Asian chess championships before. It concluded with Igor defeating Anand. Since then, they have been pitted against each other in the World Chess Championship that takes place every year. At the end of their careers, Igor was a 7-time world champion, while Anand was a 5-time world champion. Out of the 7 world championships won by Igor, he had defeated Anand in 2 of them to claim the championship title, while their other tournaments ended in a draw. In spite of being a 5-time world champion, Anand had only one regret in his life, which was not being able to defeat Igor. Finally, the opportunity Anand was waiting for had arrived.

The game of chess is completing 100 years and to mark its anniversary, FIDE, the governing body of chess, has organised a grand chess tournament. The event will be held in India, the country where the game of chess was invented during the Gupta Empire. It was originally known as 'Chaturanga', representing 4 army divisions: infantry, cavalry, elephants and chariots.

The most respected grandmasters from all over the world will be competing against each other to celebrate the success of chess as a game. While it is going to be a wonderful occasion for retired grandmasters to relive their passion, Anand saw it as a golden opportunity to defeat Igor.

"Igor Petrov. Good to see you after a very long time," said Anand.

"Anand Iyer... I think you came here for me and not for chess," replied Igor.

"Well, both chess and Igor became an exciting combination for me when we met for the first time," said Anand.

"Of course. I remember the first time we met. It was 30 years ago at the under-18 international chess tournament," replied Igor.

"So, are you excited for the chess tournament today?" questioned Anand.

"Do you mean excited to defeat you once again?" questioned Igor.

"Hehehe… we will see that, Igor. A lot has changed in all these years," said Anand.

After a short while, as all grandmasters arrived, John Hardy, the organiser and a senior member of FIDE, made an announcement.

"A very warm welcome to the best grandmasters in the world. As you all know, we are celebrating 100 years of chess today and I am very happy to see such active participation. The tournament is about to begin after 10 minutes and the pairs are as follows…" announced John.

There were a total of 7 pairs of grandmasters. Each pair had 2 grandmasters competing against each other and the pairs were created by the members of FIDE. After announcing 6 pairs, John announced the final pair, which was Anand and Igor. Everyone present at the event got super excited.

The most well-known chess rivals were going to compete against each other once again. Anand and Igor had both expected that they would be paired together. When Anand had received his invite for the event, he had made a personal request to FIDE to have Igor as his opponent. Respecting Anand and the fact that the tournament is going to take place in his own country, FIDE agreed as it will also make the event more exciting because their rivalry was a very popular one. Igor also understood before attending the event that he would be pitted against Anand, as everyone from FIDE, the grandmaster association, the audience and die hard chess fans were desperate to see them together and it was a global demand in the world of chess.

So, the chess tournament began. Igor made a powerful start by defeating Anand's knight after a few moves in the beginning, but Anand too bounced back with a powerful attack on the well-guarded king of Igor by defeating a rook and a bishop. The game became more intense with every passing minute. Many expected that the game might end in a draw position, but Anand and Igor were clear that winning is the only option for them. As time passed, the game became more intense, with Anand suffering some major losses while Igor continuously making attempts to checkmate Anand.

As the game was about to conclude, everyone present at the event was mentally transported to the world of 64 squares. It was clear that Igor is in a winning position after giving 3 back-to-back checks to Anand. To save his king, Anand had to sacrifice his queen, which was his most valuable asset. After 3-4 moves, Anand placed his knight in a new position and announced, "Checkmate". Igor noticed that his king is surrounded by a pawn, knight and bishop with no chance to escape. Anand had finally defeated Igor and satisfied his long-standing desire after decades. Everyone was shocked. Igor never saw that coming, as he was constantly pressurising Anand to defend, but Anand had smartly planned a parallel attack strategy to defeat Igor.

Post the tournament, Anand Iyer was felicitated with the '100 Years of Chess - Champion' trophy and a certificate of honour by FIDE. While Anand received a standing ovation from all chess grandmasters and the audience for his victory, the news of Anand defeating Igor spread all over the world through the internet. The tournament videos went viral on social media and many amateur chess players were trying to learn from them. The event concluded with a grand chess themed cake cutting ceremony, felicitation of all grandmasters, followed by a lavish buffet dinner.

As they were about to depart, Igor approached Anand.

"How did you manage to defeat me? Something like this has never happened before," questioned Igor.

"Igor, I told you not to take an early retirement from chess. I continued to participate and won 2 World Chess Championships after you retired. Every time I emerged as a winner, I learned something new. During my free time, I studied your method of playing very carefully. Every move, every piece, every victory and the position of your pieces every time you said checkmate. After years of study, passion to win and a strong desire to defeat you, I finally achieved my goal," explained Anand.

"Even though the feeling of losing is painful, I am happy that I got defeated by Anand Iyer, the man who belongs to the country of chess," replied Igor.

"Win, lose or draw, every time we played, the constant pressure to win against a strong player pushed both of us to grow, improve and excel in chess. Just look at our journey. We started as young players in an under-18 international chess tournament and today we are world champions of chess and the most respected grandmasters. The game becomes super exciting when you are pitted against someone as excellent as you are because, in the long run, both emerge as winners," explained Anand.

"I completely agree, Anand. What a journey it has been. Wishing you the best in life," said Igor.

"Thanks, Igor. Wishing you the same," replied Anand.

Competition has often been criticised for implying extreme pressure to win, developing a feeling of hatred against opponents and leading to a defeating situation that results in depression. At the same time, it has a brighter side too. Competing against powerful opponents is a great opportunity for valuable experience, constant improvement and an inspiration to win in life.

Final Round

In the highly competitive world of banking and finance, there are many top-notch professionals who make themselves stand apart from the crowd. They are completely prepared to battle it out when it comes to grabbing leadership roles in organisations with a strong global footprint. BFC Bank is one of the largest financial organisations in the world, having its presence in more than 150 countries, with its global headquarters based in the United Kingdom. India is the largest market for them in Asia. At present, they are headhunting for a Chief Executive Officer (CEO) who can grow their business and manage their clients in India.

Richard Watson, Global Head of Operations and Jane Casey, Head of Human Resources at BFC Bank, are currently in India to finalise the candidate. Out of 23 outstanding applications, only 3 have been shortlisted for the final round of interview. Each of them has an impressive track record and has excelled in all key parameters such as qualifications, skills, relevant experience, delivering the best results and leading with passion. The biggest challenge for Richard and Jane is to select the right man for the role. After detailed internal discussions, both of them agreed to go for a tie-breaker by asking the same question to all 3 shortlisted candidates in the final round.

Candidate 1: Naman Jain

Richard: What is your biggest achievement in life?

Naman: I have excelled in every role, organisation and challenge given to me. From winning multiple awards for quarterly and annual performance to being promoted the maximum number of times within the shortest period, I have repeatedly proved that I am better than the best. I have always been a knowledge bank with all the required information and regular updates in the industry, be it recent changes in RBI guidelines or amendments in the Indian tax structure. In my career of more than 2 decades, I have worked with startups where I initiated finance processes from scratch and established everything on my own and I have also worked with the biggest players in the banking industry, where I proved my worth in the most challenging situations that I came across. My ability to excel, strong background in the world of banking and in-depth understanding of the Indian finance industry make me the best candidate for this role.

Candidate 2: Anil Gupta

Richard: What is your biggest achievement in life?

Anil: I have been an outstanding leader. When it comes to managing teams, business verticals, or entire operations of a large-scale organisation in the banking industry, I have repeatedly proved my worth in every scenario. From being repeatedly featured in the '40 Under 40' list of India's most powerful leaders to being named the best leader in the banking industry by top corporate publications, I have a strong positive presence in the Indian BFSI industry, which defines my worth. I am the most recommended and preferred man for leadership roles in the banking industry. I have scaled organisations not only in terms of business but also in terms of managing people. Under my leadership, my organisation had the highest employee retention rate; we were named the best organisation to work for in the banking sector; we had maximum productivity and the best quality in terms of delivering output; and we launched new products, services and business units, which resulted in rapid growth and expansion of the bank.

Candidate 3: Vinit Agarwal

Richard: What is your biggest achievement in life?

Vinit: I am a self-made man. Everything I have achieved in my life so far is completely on my own. I have never used any personal, professional, or social connections to get a job or progress in my profession. I have not even taken any kind of help from any third party and have completely rejected nepotism. Even in the worst situations, when I was about to lose my job due to a shutdown or an acquisition, I took up my next role on my own. Right from my first job to my present one, I have climbed the ladder of success completely on a merit basis. I have delivered results, proved my worth and made change happen. The impact of my work speaks more than my words. My father, Aditya Agarwal, is a chartered accountant and he has his own well-established CA firm, APA & Co. After completing my studies, I had the option of joining my father's company, as it was a ready-made successful venture for me to inherit, but I opted for the hard way instead. From being shortlisted to selected to promoted, from small to medium to large and now global, achieving everything on my own is one of the best feelings I have in my life. When I look at my journey so far, I feel proud of the fact that I am a self-made man.

Richard and Jane had a detailed discussion after carefully evaluating the answers of all 3 candidates. While Jane had shortlisted 2 of them, it was Richard who finalised the right man for the role.

Jane: So, who is the face of BFC Bank in India and why?

Richard: Vinit Agarwal. I am extremely impressed by his biggest achievement of being a self-made man and it created a deep impact on my mind. While the achievements of Naman and Anil are professional in nature, Vinit's achievement is professional, personal and moral. Of course, in certain aspects, Naman and Anil were better and Vinit might have his own negatives, but no one is perfect. We don't need the best person for this role; we need a balanced one. Vinit is that one. I am confident BFC Bank will excel under his leadership in India.

The next day, Jane called Vinit and informed him that he had been selected as the CEO of BFC Bank in India. After discussing the compensation and date of joining with Jane, Vinit received his offer letter. It was not just a document for him. It was one more victory as he continued his merit-based journey of success.

Many emerge as winners in this highly competitive world, but a few of them always stand apart from others. They are the self-made ones. With their firm belief in merit and passion to win, they succeed in making a mark of their own. These self-made people are respected wherever they go, have a massive fan following, inspire others and people look up to them as their role models.

Wanderlust

Vikram Chopra has spent more than a decade of his life working with high profile technology companies. From launching new digital products to helping large scale organisations undergo digital transformation, from leading teams to training and onboarding partners with new products, technologies and feature upgrades, Vikram has done it all. His professional life has been so hectic that weekends and paid leaves were occupied with doing household work, grocery shopping and occasionally catching up with family relatives.

On a fine Monday morning, the CTO of the organisation where Vikram works made an unexpected announcement. He informed that their organisation is permanently shutting down as they were not able to manage the operational costs and growing demands of clients due to recent changes in emerging technologies. All employees will receive severance pay for 6 months. Vikram was shocked. In spite of being completely devoted to his profession and giving his best, all of a sudden, things came to an end for him.

Due to the economic slowdown, Vikram was not able to get a new job. After making a few attempts and having all the required skills, experience and knowledge, he could not make the cut. That is when he decided to go on a break. Vikram took the call that he would completely disconnect himself from work, his profession and the entire corporate world. He would go on a soul-searching journey, travelling around the world, exploring it, attempting the unattempted and experiencing life like never before.

Packing his bags with all the required essentials, including his high resolution digital camera, Vikram had only one thing in his mind: no matter what happens, he will do everything he had mentioned in his bucket list. Since the break is going to be a long one, Vikram had planned everything in advance, right from the first place of visit to the last one. Finally, his much awaited journey began.

In the first 3 months of his exploration, Vikram visited some of the most popular tourist attractions in the world, from Machu Picchu in Peru to the Matterhorn in Switzerland. He observed how the professional, personal and social life of people differs based on the country they live in and its geographical location. In one corner of this world were the countries with rich history like Italy, while in the other corner were completely modernised countries like Singapore and then there were countries like India, which were more diverse than an entire continent. Vikram was particularly impressed by the fact that the world offers so much to someone with wanderlust.

During his journey, Vikram also took part in many adventure activities like paragliding and snorkeling. He interacted with locals of the respective countries, celebrated their festivals and tried out their food, drinks, clothing and lifestyle. While Vikram experienced life like never before, he was also expanding his knowledge of how external factors like climate, surroundings and local pop culture affect the way of living. As Vikram wanted to share his journey, experiences and discoveries with others, he actively posted all his ongoing activities on his Instagram page 'Wanderlust Vikram'. From photos and reels of must visit places to live video streaming of exciting activities and festive celebrations, tagging their locations in each of his posts for his followers.

Vikram decided his final destination will be in his own country, India. The reason for it was a newly inaugurated place which had gained a lot of national as well as international recognition and not many people in India had experienced it before, as it was something new. Vikram wanted to be one of the early locals to visit the place and share his experience with all his followers, which had tripled during his entire journey because of the pictures, videos and experiences he shared. So his final destination was none other than the Statue of Unity. With a height of 182 meters, the Statue of Unity has already been registered in the Guinness World Records as the tallest statue in the world and has been added to the 8 Wonders of the Shanghai Cooperation Organisation list. Upon reaching the site, Vikram explored the giant statue from outside, went inside it and took an elevator to the viewing gallery which gives a panoramic view of the Sardar Sarovar Dam, he also visited the valley of flowers close by and enjoyed the stunning laser show at night marking an end to his journey.

Vikram was finally back home. Home sweet home. Happy and satisfied with the feeling of having completed his wishlist, doing everything he had always wanted to for a very long time. As Vikram was going through his Instagram page 'Wanderlust Vikram', he came across a DM in his inbox. It was from someone named Danica Diaz. In her message, Danica mentioned that she wanted to meet Vikram to discuss an exciting opportunity with him. Vikram immediately replied and their meeting was fixed.

Vikram and Danica met as decided. Danica revealed that she works for Beta, which is one of the largest digital video platforms in the world with more than 80 million paid subscribers. Beta is planning to launch a travel show in a very unique format on its platform. The show is going to be titled 'Explore the Unexplored', which will cover all the unique places and hidden gems in the world that are not popular among tourists. 'Explore the Unexplored' aims to spread awareness and share experiences about out-of-the-box locations that are often skipped by the majority of people. Having closely observed the fast-growing popularity of Vikram's Instagram page 'Wanderlust Vikram', with more than a million followers, Beta has shortlisted Vikram as the host for 'Explore the Unexplored'. Upon carefully going through the entire offer, Vikram immediately agreed to host the show. Beta offered an attractive package to Vikram along with amazing benefits and an opportunity to explore and experience places never seen before around the world.

'Explore the Unexplored' became an instant hit in its first week of release, with the highest streaming count on the Beta platform. The production team of the show is now planning a second season and they have extended Vikram's contract. Vikram has also received many other offers for new shows and he is now a super busy man with opportunities that are exciting and rewarding. Life completely changed for him and the second phase of his career has proved to be way better than the first one. This unexpected change took place because Vikram Chopra was consumed by wanderlust.

Every person in this world is occupied with a daily routine and at a certain stage, life becomes remote controlled. It is extremely important to occasionally take a break in life. This major disconnection from everything else marks a new beginning. One must explore the world, try out new things, gain the most unique, out of the box experiences and rediscover life. Such diverse global exposure will result in a massive transformation of character and overall personality. The comeback of such a person will be much more powerful, impactful and inspiring.

Jigsaw Puzzle

At times, life seems very confusing. A person finds it extremely difficult to make a choice. Which choice will be an appropriate one or prove beneficial in the long run is always difficult to decide. In such cases, people generally prefer to go with the majority, but there are a few who choose their own path.

Anaisha is an 8-year-old cute, bubbly girl next door. She is a single child and does not have any siblings. As a result, she used to spend her free time outside her home. Every day in the evening, Anaisha used to visit the park next to her home, enjoying the company of flowers, the lawn, birds, fresh air and her special friend Masterji, who is a 70-year-old retired school teacher. Anaisha and Masterji had become close friends within a short span of time as they used to live in the same locality and visited the park daily.

While Anaisha is a curious girl who wants to know more about life, Masterji enjoyed sharing his knowledge even after his teaching profession concluded a decade ago. A man whose life is about to end and a girl whose life has just begun, Masterji and Anaisha shared a very special and unique bond.

Anaisha was always confused about her future. What will happen? What will she become? What will she achieve? Will she be able to make her parents proud? With a growing number of extended family members and relatives questioning her about her future plans and encouraging her to be ambitious in life, Anaisha was unable to figure out her life and decided to discuss it with Masterji.

"Masterji, when you were of my age, did you have any ambition in life?" questioned Anaisha.

"Not at all, Anaisha. In fact, I was just happy playing around at home," replied Masterji.

"Then why is everyone asking me about my future plans and what I want to become when I grow up?" questioned Anaisha.

"I think you are still too young to decide. People question you because this world has become much more competitive than it was during my time. Everybody wants progress within a short span of time. But you should not give much importance to such questions," replied Masterji.

"I have decided that I need to have an ambition in life. What do you think will be the best profession for me in the future?" questioned Anaisha.

"I can't say that, Anaisha. When I was your age, I had no idea I would become a teacher in the future. As a child, I enjoyed sharing knowledge with others. As I grew up, I started training and guiding those who were younger than me. When everybody gave me positive feedback about my skills, I decided to take up teaching as a profession. In my career of more than 30 years, I have taught thousands and my students have become doctors, chartered accountants, entrepreneurs and even navy officers. I never told my students what they should become in life. Instead, I told them to do what they feel happy doing, just like me," replied Masterji.

"Masterji, I don't know what makes me happy. I am confused and unable to decide," said Anaisha.

Masterji took out a small box from his bag and gave it to Anaisha. When Anaisha opened the box, she saw cardboard pieces of different shapes with different images printed on each one of them. Anaisha picked up a single piece and examined it carefully. Masterji explained the practical assignment he had planned for her.

"Anaisha, this is a jigsaw puzzle. I often play it during my spare time. It is a single-player board game where you have to connect all the pieces as per their appropriate interlocks. When all the pieces are connected in the right order, it will form an image. Solve this puzzle and bring it the next time we meet," said Masterji.

An excited Anaisha went running back home and immersed herself in solving the jigsaw puzzle. She started with the most colourful piece and then soon found three interconnecting pieces in a row. After placing a few wrong pieces, then removing and replacing them again, Anaisha started gaining confidence. There was also an eagerness and excitement in her to find out what the puzzle would reveal. After observing the images and patterns of the pieces carefully, Anaisha finally succeeded in connecting all the pieces in the right order. The puzzle was solved and it revealed an image of Mount Everest. The next day, Anaisha presented the entire connected cardboard to Masterji.

"Wow… you solved the jigsaw puzzle within a day. That was quick and unexpected, Anaisha," said Masterji.

"Thank you, Masterji," replied Anaisha.

"How did you solve this puzzle?" asked Masterji.

"Well, I started with the piece which I liked the most. Then I found three other pieces of the sequence in a row. I kept on arranging and rearranging the pieces. When I failed, I figured out my mistake and tried again. When I succeeded to some extent, I became confident about my next move and managed to solve the entire puzzle. I just did what I felt was right," replied Anaisha.

"Exactly. This is how we solve the jigsaw puzzle of life. In the beginning, things appear confusing just like the pieces of a puzzle. Identify your area of interest and start with what you like doing the most. Proceed ahead step by step. Do what you feel is right. Listen to your mind, heart and soul. If you fail, you will learn something new and if you succeed, you will keep moving forward. In the end, you will finally reach the peak of your life," Masterji concluded as he pointed his finger at the peak of Mount Everest in the image.

"Now I feel much better than before. Thank you, Masterji," replied Anaisha.

15 years later…

At the grand finale of Served Hot, the most popular national cooking competition, a signature dish was prepared by each of the finalists. After a detailed discussion among the jury panel, the host made the announcement everyone was eagerly waiting for.

"The title of 'Served Hot Chef of the Year' goes to Anaisha. Her dish has been the most innovative one. A perfect mixture of nutritious ingredients and taste like never experienced before, Anaisha has also given equal importance to factors like freshness and unique presentation. What's more? She is the youngest contestant to win this title. Extraordinary indeed. I request her to come on stage and collect the award," said the host.

After collecting her award, Anaisha went on to share her experience and journey so far.

"Thank you. This is like a dream come true for me. I started developing a keen interest in food as it is a part of our daily lives. Since most girls these days have stepped out of the kitchen and opted for academically inclined professions, I decided to do the reverse and step into the kitchen. Being a foodie, I enjoyed experimenting with different ingredients and flavours. Indian cuisine is the most diverse cuisine in the world and it offers a huge scope for innovation. While every region of India has its own specialty, it also opened doors for me to create fusion dishes which were a blend of different cultures. Combining all these factors, I became passionate about cooking and decided to become a chef. My family was completely against my decision, as the current generation of women is busy working in the corporate world, but I just did what I enjoyed the most and here I am today. All this was possible because of one man, my special friend, mentor and guide… Masterji. I dedicate this award to him," concluded Anaisha.

The next day, Masterji received a parcel at his home. He unpacked it and found a jigsaw puzzle inside it. He connected the pieces of the puzzle and it revealed a picture of Anaisha winning the 'Served Hot Chef of the Year' award. Masterji quickly called Anaisha and congratulated her. It was a happy and memorable moment for him during last moments of his life.

In life, we always find it difficult to make a choice. People give their opinions, warn about the unexpected path that lies ahead and generally tell you to go with the flow. But only those who opt for the odd ones become successful.

They emerge as winners because they always follow their mind, heart and soul. Don't do what others say. Just listen and learn from them. Do what you feel is right.

Lights, Camera, Action!

A director is like the CEO of a movie. He has complete control over all stages of the filmmaking process such as pre-production, production and post-production. He is in charge of all aspects of a film such as script, screenplay, music, choreography, editing and so on. It is the most challenging role in the film industry. It is the director who initiates the filming process by giving the standard cue to his cast and crew when he shouts, “Lights, camera, action!”

Sujoy Mukherjee has directed more than 25 films till date and all of them have been blockbusters at the box office, won national and international awards and were critically acclaimed by industry experts. Sujoy made films that appealed to each and every person irrespective of age group, gender, caste, community or region. His films reflected humour, simplicity and humanity. His latest release, Parvarish, highlights the importance of parenting for the growth and development of a child. After the success of his every film, Sujoy Mukherjee organises a get together for the cast and crew of his film. At the success celebrations of Parvarish, Sujoy made an announcement.

"First of all, I would like to thank each and every one of you for your valuable contribution in making Parvarish. For me, every movie is like a dream which I have to turn into reality. Today, my dream has turned into reality and I am able to share it with everyone on the big screen. This is possible just because of my entire cast and crew. You all were completely devoted to your respective tasks, committed to delivering within the given time frame by using your expertise to deliver the best quality. We have all been working together like a family for a very long time and will continue to do so. Cheers to many more successful films in the future."

As Sujoy Mukherjee concluded his speech, his cinematographer, Manish approached him for a personal conversation.

"Sujoy sir, I have been working with you for more than 12 years and I have always observed that you continue to work with the same cast and crew members instead of hiring a new cast and crew for every film like other film directors. Why is your approach different from others?" questioned Manish.

"Because my entire cast and crew have performed consistently over these years. Why should I bring in new people when there is nothing wrong with my current ones? My past record of successful films is a living testimonial to the fact that I have the best talent in the Indian film industry. Well, you can say my loyalty towards them is a reward for their successful track record," explained Sujoy.

“Thank you, Sujoy sir. We are blessed to have a director like you in the Indian film industry. We are all looking forward to starting work on your next film Golu ki Gaadi,” said Manish.

“The script and screenplay for Golu ki Gaadi are ready. We will begin shooting for the film next month, so prepare yourself for our next film,” said Sujoy.

Sujoy Mukherjee's next film Golu ki Gaadi was about a boy named Golu who hails from a middle class family and dreams of having his own car. The shooting of the film was completed in 3 months, followed by post-production work and the film was released during the festive season. Sujoy Mukherjee and his entire cast and crew were looking forward to the audience response.

All of a sudden, the most unexpected thing happened. Golu ki Gaadi flopped at the box office. The audience went for the film with high expectations and the film turned out to be disappointing. In fact, the word of mouth and reviews of Golu ki Gaadi were so negative that there was a huge drop in the box office collections right from the second day of its release, in spite of the festive season. Sujoy Mukherjee was completely shocked and depressed as he failed to live up to everyone's expectations.

Post the failure of Golu ki Gaadi, Sujoy's credibility as a director was put in doubt. Many producers cancelled their future collaborations with him, while many turned their backs on him due to insecurity. Everyone concluded that Sujoy had lost his ability to create magic on the big screen.

After a short break, Sujoy Mukherjee, along with his team of writers, created a script with an innovative theme for his next film titled Suhana Safar, but he found it extremely difficult to find a producer for it. He also approached many media corporations, but they too turned down his script. Finally, Sujoy decided to self-finance his own film, for which he approached a bank for a loan. Since making a film is an expensive and time consuming process with a heavy risk of failure, the bank rejected his loan application. Sujoy tried every possible approach, but nobody showed faith in his project.

After a few days, Manish, the cinematographer working for Sujoy, called him up and requested him for a personal meeting at his home. Later, when Sujoy arrived at his home, he was surprised to see his entire cast and crew: actors, singers, scriptwriters, editors, music directors, choreographers, costume designers and so on. Manish began the conversation on a warm note.

"Sujoy sir, there is news in the film industry that you are not able to make financial arrangements for your next film, Suhana Safar. We have all decided that we will not charge any fees from you for making Suhana Safar. We all will completely support you in making the entire film and releasing it," announced Manish.

"Thank you for your support, but I can't let this happen. I mean, it will be so unfair on my part to utilise your skills and not reward you for the same. Sorry, I cannot accept this proposal," replied Sujoy.

"Sujoy sir, you have always shared your success with us and repeatedly mentioned that we all have equally contributed to making all your past films a huge success. In the same way, if Golu ki Gaadi flopped, it indicates that we were all equally responsible for its failure. Then why is it only you who is suffering? If you can share your success with us, you should also share your failure with us. We humbly request that you consider our proposal. Let us prove once again that one flop movie cannot affect our passion for making the finest cinema," explained Manish.

After giving it some thought, Sujoy Mukherjee agreed to accept the proposal offered to him by everyone. Lights, camera, action! The shooting for Suhana Safar begins. It is a film about two friends who go on a road trip to explore rural life in different regions of India. Suhana Safar presented the diversity of rural India in an innovative way, highlighting cultural aspects of each region such as food, dress attire, festivals, wedding rituals, etc. The entire cast and crew got completely involved in making the film. Many cast and crew members also contributed money for minor costs such as costumes, equipment and other supportive gear. Sujoy Mukherjee himself funded the film from his personal savings. The film was completed and released in theatres as scheduled.

Suhana Safar emerged as a blockbuster. A huge box office success. The audience enjoyed watching the road trip across rural India. Even 3 months after its release, all the shows were houseful. It was the lowest budget film directed by Sujoy Mukherjee, which generated maximum revenue for him as the project was self-financed. Sujoy also received a whopping amount from a leading TV channel for the broadcast rights of Suhana Safar. Many film producers acquired remake rights of Suhana Safar for their respective regional cinemas, which generated more revenue than Sujoy ever expected.

As a part of his tradition of celebrating success, during the get together of Suhana Safar, Sujoy Mukherjee announced that he will be paying the entire fees to each and every cast and crew member from the huge revenues generated by the film. Further, Sujoy added that he will also be paying an additional bonus amount to everyone for supporting his film in the most difficult times and making the impossible happen. The entire cast and crew gave a standing ovation to Sujoy Mukherjee for his kind gesture.

A true leader is one who always motivates his people, appreciates their good work, gives regular feedbacks for improvement and shares his success with everyone. At the same time, every individual needs to understand the importance of having an inspiring leader and support him in his vision. If everybody works with such a positive approach, even in the most difficult situations, the impossible can be achieved.

Doctor's Dilemma

Dr. Akshay Parikh is a top notch cardiologist. Known for his expertise in successfully executing the most complicated and complex heart surgeries, Dr. Akshay Parikh holds a record of saving all his patients from the jaws of death. Even in the medical fraternity, everyone from the most skilled and experienced doctors to young students studying at top medical institutions in India follows his guidance, reads his books and never fails to attend his seminars on cardiology. The Medical Council of India recently elected him as their next chairman after being impressed by his extraordinary achievements in medical science.

It was just another normal day for Dr. Parikh when he left for the hospital. On his way, he had no idea that one of the most challenging cases of his life is waiting for him, where his abilities would be tested at an extreme level. Upon reaching the hospital, nurse Jyoti informed him that his appointment scheduled with Ravi Raichand, the owner of Raichand Textiles, to discuss the complicated case of his father, Prakash Raichand. Dr. Parikh entered the meeting room and saw Ravi Raichand with his father, Prakash Raichand, eagerly waiting for him.

"Good morning, Dr. Parikh. Finally got a chance to meet the best of the best. It is a dream come true to meet you in person," said Ravi.

"Thank you for your kind words, Mr. Raichand. So, how can I help you?" asked Dr. Parikh.

"This is my father, Prakash Raichand. He is 80 years old and often gets minor heart attacks. He also has other issues like chest pain and high blood pressure at times. With every passing day, the pain is becoming unbearable for him. I want you to help him get rid of his pain. My father has always been a kind hearted and generous man. Our entire Raichand family looks up to him as an inspiration. All our family members take his guidance on professional, personal and social issues of life and he has been like a perfect mentor to everyone. We really need him," explained Ravi.

Dr. Parikh physically examined Prakashji and conducted a few medical checks, after which he informed Ravi that the condition is serious and his father needed to undergo surgery within a week. Ravi quickly gave a go ahead to Dr. Parikh. The date for the operation was finalised and the entire process was explained to Prakashji and Ravi in advance. As they were leaving for the day, Prakashji requested to have a private talk with Dr. Parikh. As Ravi left the room, Prakashji expressed his desire to Dr. Parikh.

"Dr. Parikh, I know you have a record of saving the lives of each and every patient of yours, but deeply, from the bottom of my heart, I request you to break your record. Please don't save me during my operation," said Prakashji.

Dr. Parikh was shocked. Completely silent for a few minutes, not able to utter even a word. He had never come across such a situation in his career so far.

"Prakashji, you have a happy life, supportive and caring family members who want you to live. They want you to celebrate every day of life with them. Why do you want to end your life?" questioned Dr. Parikh.

"Because the end of life is a law of nature. Every human is born to die. On the other hand, the pain of my poor health has become unbearable for me. Regular consumption of medicines, occasional surgeries, internal body pain and external weakness. It is just too much. Even though my children and family members say that I am not a burden on them, I firmly believe I am. They have spent so much time, money and resources on me. All this for what? Just so that I can die another day? My life is already over. I did everything that I could do for myself and my family. Now I want the next generation of the Raichand family to take over completely and do the same. That is how the life cycle goes on. Please end my life," concluded Prakash Raichand.

"Then why did you not express this desire to your family members? Why did you come to me?" questioned Dr. Parikh.

"Because they will think I am committing suicide. This is not suicide. Ending your life at a time when it is about to end is a personal choice. Also, if I commit suicide, it will demotivate my family members and they will think I was depressed and unhappy with my life, which is clearly not the case. I want my death to appear natural. I want to leave this world on a positive note," said Prakashji.

"Give me some time to decide on what needs to be done in your case. I will get back to you within a day, Prakashji," replied Dr. Parikh.

"Sure. When you take your final decision, just keep one thing in mind: even if you don't save me, you will still be a lifesaver. Fulfilling the last wish of a dying man is an act of generosity," said Prakashji as he left the room.

On his way back home, Dr. Parikh faced a dilemma like never before. While it is very common for doctors to come across such situations in their profession, this one was very different. On one side was his oath to protect every patient and his life saving record and on the other side was a dying man's wish to relieve him permanently from unbearable pain.

Dr. Parikh thought a lot about the situation the whole evening and the whole night. He did a careful analysis of the situation and what the possible outcome would be. He also conducted a detailed case study to work out what would be best for everyone. Finally, he arrived at a logical conclusion and called Prakashji the next day to inform him of his decision.

"Prakashji, I have finally arrived at a conclusion that we will proceed ahead as per the outcome suggested by you. I am scheduling your heart surgery for Friday. Please inform your elder son, Ravi, to be here. Kindly note that we don't allow more than 2 family members of the patient in the hospital during the operation," said Dr. Parikh.

Post the conversation, Prakash Raichand was completely satisfied. He never had any complaints about anything and he made a few final arrangements for himself and his family members without anyone's knowledge.

On the day of Prakash Raichand's operation, he was accompanied to the hospital by his son Ravi Raichand and his wife. While both of them patiently waited in the corridor, inside the operation theatre, Prakash Raichand personally thanked Dr. Parikh for considering his last wish and gave him a tight hug before he initiated the surgery.

After an hour, Dr. Parikh stepped out of the operation theatre and informed Ravi that his father is no more. As Ravi broke down completely, his wife tried to calm him. For the rest of the hospital staff, the news was a big shock. For the first time, someone died under Dr. Parikh's supervision. Considering Dr.

Parikh's past record, nobody questioned him. Everyone, including Ravi Raichand, believed that Dr. Parikh made his best attempt to save Prakashji. Ravi thanked Dr. Parikh for taking up the challenging case of his father and for his efforts to save him.

Years later, Dr. Akshay Parikh retired from the medical profession. However, he continued to teach cardiology to young medical students as a visiting faculty, explaining the most complex heart surgeries executed by him and sharing his experiences in the field of medical science. Once, a medical student questioned him in one of his lectures about the only time he failed to save a life.

"Sir, tell us about the only case of yours where the patient died. How did you feel when you failed to retain your record of being a guaranteed lifesaver?" questioned the student.

Dr. Parikh smiled and replied:

"Life and death of a person are not controlled by doctors. We try our level best to save a life. Every single time I entered the operation theatre, I was committed to my oath of saving my patient so that he could experience the gift of nature called life. The case of Prakash Raichand was not a failure for me. Prakashji was living an extremely painful life with a rapid approach towards death. In spite of my best efforts, when I failed to save him, I did not feel bad. I believe I saved Prakash Raichand from a painful life. Hence, I did retain my record of being a guaranteed lifesaver."

Post Dr. Parikh's reply, all medical students gave him a standing ovation as they understood the challenging situations they will face in the future and how to deal with them in a positive way.

Every person faces a dilemma at a certain stage in life. Such a situation is extremely challenging, as one has to make a difficult choice from the available options. To overcome such a dilemma, one needs to keep emotions and moral values aside and think logically, considering the present situation and its possible outcome in the future.

Timekeeper

Time is the primary component of life. Right from birth to death, the entire life of a person is measured in time. Time defines childhood, youth, old age and personal events of life such as birthdays and anniversaries. Hence, many people in this world give utmost importance to time. They respect time and plan everything keeping time in mind. These people are known as timekeepers.

Darshit Joshi is a dedicated timekeeper. Punctuality is like an addiction to him. His entire life is driven by time. Darshit is a firm believer in the concept of early to bed, early to rise makes a man healthy, wealthy and wise. His daily schedule is planned in advance; he hates being late and strictly follows his timetable in daily life. Whenever someone questions Darshit about his time addiction, he clearly says that the whole world respects those who respect time. Darshit has been able to achieve a lot in life by being an excellent timekeeper and that was when he decided to make time his profession.

Darshit Joshi is self-employed and has been successfully running his company 'Always on Time' for the past 8 years. Always on Time is a completely time-driven company where they deliver products, offer services and provide assistance exactly at the time requested by the client. Starting from just 3 clients, today the company has more than 300 clients. Darshit himself manages the portfolio of his key clients, who are seasoned and the primary source of high revenue for Always on Time. The rest of the clients are equally distributed among the timekeeper agents who are trained to plan and execute different scenarios. A few such scenarios include delivery of gifts at the venue on time, helping students reach their exam centre on time and transport of high value cargo at a railway station, airport or shipyard on time.

On a bright Friday morning, Mr. Mirani, a key client of Always on Time, called up Darshit.

"Good morning, Darshit," said Mr. Mirani.

"Good morning, Mr. Mirani. So what is my new task?" questioned Darshit, as he is always excited to take up time based work.

"Hahaha… I like this spirit of yours. Well, I am celebrating my 25th marriage anniversary with my entire family on Sunday. As I am completing the silver jubilee of my married life, I have planned to celebrate it exactly when the day begins, which is at 12:00 a.m. I have placed an order at Cake Castle bakery for a customised 25th anniversary cake as a surprise for my wife. The cake needs to be delivered exactly at 12:00 a.m. at my home. Since Cake Castle does not deliver at night and time here is very important, I need your assistance," explained Mr. Mirani.

"Thank you for considering Always on Time for your special occasion, Mr. Mirani. We will be happy to assist you as per your requirement. Can you provide me with the pick-up and delivery details?" asked Darshit.

"You already know the bakery. All you need to do is store it for a while and deliver it exactly at 12:00 a.m. at my home," answered Mr. Mirani.

"Sounds good. Your anniversary cake will reach you at 12:00 a.m., Mr. Mirani," replied Darshit.

"Thanks a lot, Darshit. You have always been on time in all my past assignments and I respect you a lot for your time based commitment and execution skills. Will see you at 12:00 a.m.," said Mr. Mirani and disconnected the call.

Darshit decided to execute the task himself rather than assigning it to his timekeeper agents, as it was a weekend, the delivery was going to be at midnight, the occasion is a special one and above all, Mr. Mirani is a key client of Always on Time.

On Saturday night, Darshit left for his destination with the marriage anniversary cake as per his schedule. On the way, he took a shortcut through an internal lane to avoid traffic. While passing through the lane, he was forcibly stopped by a man who was standing in the middle of the road. The man was extremely tense as he approached Darshit.

"Hello, young man. My name is Vijay Singh. I have a flight to catch and need to reach the airport on time. I left early from home, but my taxi had a flat tyre on the way. Because of the weekend and this place being disconnected from the main road, I need a lift. Please help me out; this is extremely urgent," requested Vijay.

Darshit gave it a thought. In front of his eyes is a punctual man like him who is a victim of bad timing. He needed to be on time, or else he would miss his flight, which would have a negative effect on his schedule. Since the airport is on his way, Darshit decided to help him out. Vijay quickly took his baggage and joined Darshit in his car. Darshit and Vijay both had a brief interaction on the way, where Darshit informed Vijay about his time-based business, Always on Time. Soon, the duo reached the airport and Vijay thanked Darshit for his help, after which he rushed towards the flight counter to collect his boarding pass.

While departing from the airport, Darshit got caught up in a traffic jam as a flight had recently landed and many passengers had hired taxis to reach their destinations. The airport exit was blocked. This traffic resulted in a delay for Darshit. As Darshit already knew that he would not be able to make it on time at Mr. Mirani's home, he took a halt at Cheers, which is one of the largest liquor shops in the city. Darshit purchased M&N wine as a gift for Mr. Mirani to compensate for the delay. He finally reached Mr. Mirani's home. It was 12:20 a.m. He was 20 minutes late. Darshit saw a disappointed Mr. Mirani standing at the entrance of his home. He quickly stepped out of his car and approached him.

"I am extremely sorry for the delay, Mr. Mirani. I was caught up in an unexpected situation on my way," said Darshit.

"In the past, you have always been on time, Darshit. This is the first time something like this has happened. I am sure you must have tried your best to be on time. It's okay, I understand," said Mr. Mirani.

"Thank you, Mr. Mirani. As a gesture of goodwill, I would like to gift you M&N wine. Kindly accept it," requested Darshit.

"Thank you so much, Darshit. This is an added bonus to my surprise, as my wife loves wine," said Mr. Mirani.

"Wishing you a very happy marriage anniversary, Mr. Mirani," said Darshit.

"Thank you, Darshit," replied Mr. Mirani.

On his way back home, Darshit was a bit disappointed, but it also made him realise how a small gesture of goodwill can make things right.

The next week, Darshit received a call from Vijay Singh. He got Darshit's contact details from the Always on Time website. Vijay informed him that because of his help on Saturday night, he was able to reach his destination on time and deliver the antibiotic medicines required for the emergency treatment of patients. Vijay further informed Darshit that he is the Head of Supply Chain at a leading pharmaceutical company and being impressed by his commitment towards time, he would like to sign up

Always on Time as their vaccine delivery partner. As a part of this assignment, Always on Time would be delivering vaccines at medical camps in remote locations. Darshit was extremely happy to have a new client on board. But the biggest surprise came for him in the evening.

The owner of Cheers liquor shop came to meet Darshit at his office. He informed Darshit that M&N Wines celebrated their foundation day on Sunday and since Darshit was the first customer to purchase M&N wine on their foundation day, exactly at 12:00 a.m., he had won an SUV car as a bumper prize. It was then that Darshit recollected dropping his business card while purchasing M&N wine, as requested by the shop manager. Now it became clear to him what it was all about.

As per the growing business needs of Always on Time, Darshit was planning to buy a spacious car for work purposes and his wish was granted without any cost. It happened just because he made a purchase at a particular time. After a busy weekend night, it was a great start to a new week. Darshit Joshi strongly felt he had been rewarded because of his strong commitment towards time, being punctual and being an excellent timekeeper.

Time is the most valuable aspect of life. It has been repeatedly observed that most successful people in the world have given utmost importance to time in their lives, which has resulted in making them conquer the peak. There are days when time is not in favour of a person, but at a later stage, time rewards such people for their dedication. This is why timekeepers are guaranteed winners in life.

Seal the Deal

Diamonds are the most expensive and valuable gemstones in the world and in the billion-dollar global diamond industry, India's diamond kings are the biggest players. One of them is Naksh Modi, the Managing Director of Nitara Diamonds, a 90-year-old diamond firm. Born into the third generation of an Indian diamantaire family, Naksh Modi has many top-notch clients who have been loyal to Nitara Diamonds, but the new diamond merchants entering the industry have come up with extremely lucrative offers to attract these loyal clients and seal the deal with them. Diamond debutant Rajiv Desai is one of them.

"Mohanji, I am committed to providing the finest quality of diamonds. I believe in maintaining excellence in Cut, Colour, Carat and Clarity, which are the four 'C' parameters that define the value of a diamond," said Rajiv.

"Hmmm... these diamond samples are at par with the current ones which we buy," said Mohandas after careful examination of the diamond specimens presented by Rajiv.

Mohandas Zaveri of Zaveri Jewellers is a reputed diamond jeweller known for crafting the finest quality of diamond ornaments ranging from necklaces to bracelets. When it comes to buying diamonds for his jewellery, he has been a loyal client of Nitara Diamonds, but today Rajiv Desai has made an attractive proposal as he is desperate to add Zaveri Jewellers to his portfolio of clients.

"We will provide you with all the benefits and services that you currently avail from Nitara Diamonds. In addition, we will also provide complimentary cutting and polishing services for a fixed period, insurance cover for diamonds and rare specimens of other gemstones, such as ruby and sapphire at nominal rates," said Rajiv.

"Mr. Desai, I really like your diamonds and proposal, but I am happy and completely satisfied with my current supplier, Nitara Diamonds. I wish to continue doing business with them," said Mohandas.

"Mohanji, in addition to my previous proposal, I will also showcase your jewellery catalogue on my online portal without any additional charges. This will not only expand your reach to a wider consumer base but will also generate new leads for you," said Rajiv.

"Well, that sounds great, but I am not interested," replied Mohanji.

Rajiv still believed he could change Mohandas Zaveri's decision and made one last attempt to seal the deal.

"Mohanji, apart from everything I mentioned earlier, we also have a strong presence at international diamond auctions. If you accept my proposal, I will showcase your jewellery at the most respected auctions and based on the bidding process, you will get a much higher price for your diamond ornaments. This is also a lifetime opportunity for you to go global," said Rajiv.

"Mr. Desai, after considering all your services and benefits, I wish to inform you that I am not interested in your offer. I have always done business with Nitara Diamonds and will continue to do so in the future. It is a special relationship that I value based on my years of experience with Naksh Modi. I am sorry," replied Mohandas.

A disappointed Rajiv left with a heavy heart. He was unable to figure out what went wrong. After making every move in the right direction and multiple attempts, he had failed to seal the deal. In the evening, Rajiv narrated the entire incident to his boss.

"Sir, I did everything the way you instructed me. I made multiple pitches with more tempting benefits but was unable to convince Mohandas Zaveri. I failed to seal the deal. He was firm in his decision to continue doing business with Nitara Diamonds. Where did I go wrong?" questioned Rajiv.

Naksh Modi had a sparkling smile on his face as he went through the scenario.

"You did not do anything wrong, Rajiv. I had sent you to Mohandas Zaveri in disguise as a new diamond merchant to test his loyalty towards Nitara Diamonds and get a clear picture of what my client thinks of me. Mohandas did not seal the deal offered by you because I have earned his trust through years of dedicated service. I have focused on the key parameters of the diamond trade like growth, engagement and retention. Even in the most challenging situations, I have never compromised on productivity or quality. I have conducted regular client feedback sessions and have constantly improved wherever required. During the crisis period in the diamond industry, I have suffered losses but made sure my clients made profits. When my grandfather started Nitara Diamonds, he made two rules. First rule: Don't take your clients for granted and never lose their trust. Second rule: Don't break the first rule. I belong to the third generation in my family managing Nitara Diamonds and I am very happy that all these years we have retained our core values," concluded Naksh.

This is the best example of self-appraisal. In the fast-changing world with cut throat competition, if you want to be on top and retain your position, you need to constantly evaluate yourself and maintain perfection. If you don't fight for what you want, then don't cry for what you lost.

Fail

There is one word that every person fears in life: FAIL. The fear of failure and its after effects have been extremely dangerous. People get demotivated, are scared of making a second attempt, avoid trying out new things and a few of them even end their lives. But there are some who see failure in a completely different way. One of them is Abhinav Shukla.

Early in the morning, Rohan rushed as the doorbell rang to collect the daily newspaper. After grabbing it, he went through the headline on its front page, 'Abhinav Shukla wins World Cycling Championship (WCC) for the third time in a row'. Apart from the news, there is one more reason why 12-year-old Rohan is super excited. He had recently won a Facebook meet and greet contest conducted on Abhinav Shukla's official fan page. Out of more than five thousand participants, Rohan was the lucky winner and the next week he would be meeting Abhinav Shukla in person at his home.

After clearing the security check outside Abhinav's home, Rohan was escorted towards the main hall by the butler. As Rohan was desperately waiting in the main hall for Abhinav to arrive, he glanced at the exhibit area in the main room. The number of trophies in front of Rohan's eyes were more than the number of hairs on his head. From the first cycle race, which Abhinav won during his school days to his state and national level victories, to his Asian and European tour wins, followed by 3 World Cycling Championships.

As Rohan was going through the milestones achieved by Abhinav, a voice emerged from behind.

"Good morning, Rohan," said Abhinav Shukla.

"Good morning, Abhinav and congratulations on winning the WCC," replied Rohan as he saw the dashing, physically fit, stunning personality.

"Thank you, Rohan. I am blessed to have well wishing fans like you. Come join me for breakfast," said Abhinav.

It was the healthiest breakfast, ranging from fresh green salads to toast, butter, yoghurts and fruit juices. Rohan took a bowl of salad and a glass of mango juice. He decided to follow the same menu for his daily breakfast. As Rohan and Abhinav had brief interactions related to work, personal life and daily routine, Abhinav noticed a discomfort in Rohan's behaviour and questioned him about it.

"What's wrong, Rohan? You seem a bit upset," asked Abhinav.

"Abhinav, I have sports day coming up at school. Every year I used to participate in the cycle race, but this year I have decided not to. I have never won in the past and have given up hope of winning in the future. I am scared that if I fail, one more defeat will not only demotivate me but also my parents, who have high expectations from me," replied Rohan.

"Hahaha… you are scared of losing a cycle race? When I was your age, I didn't even know how to ride a cycle," said Abhinav.

"What? Then how did you conquer the world of cycling?" asked Rohan.

"Well, Rohan, I will share my secret of winning with you, but only on one condition. You will participate in the cycle race on sports day," said Abhinav.

"Done," replied Rohan immediately.

Abhinav narrates…

"The first time I made an attempt to learn how to ride a cycle was when I was 12. I still remember my first attempt. As I started pedalling, my hands were shaking, unable to control the steering handle. Within a few seconds, I lost my balance and I was lying on the ground.

After a few more failed attempts resulting in cuts, bleeding, knee and elbow injuries and no further improvements, I finally decided to quit. I could not bear the pain and falling anymore. After 2 years, when I was 14, I noticed that all children of my age in my locality, in my school and in my family knew how to ride a cycle except me.

On one side, I felt I was left behind while everyone moved ahead and on the other side, I thought if everyone can, then even I can. The feeling of being the only one who couldn't ride a cycle was more painful than my injuries. That was the time I decided that no matter how many times I fail, I will learn to ride a cycle. I started where I left off and the result was the same every time: fail, fail, fail. After multiple attempts, with elbow skin peeled off, bleeding knees and falling flat on the ground, I finally got my balance right. It took almost 3 weeks to achieve this.

After gaining complete control of the steering, brakes and pedals, I started cycling on the main road and then I began going to school on my cycle. As time passed, I got addicted to cycling. Maybe because I was a late learner and wanted to catch up. Cycling around home, cycling at school, cycling wherever I went. My non-stop cycling addiction resulted in achieving perfection and just because I enjoyed cycling, I participated in the cycle race at my school and ended up winning it. After that, there was no turning back. And look where I am today.

Just look at the most successful people from any profession. They never had an easy life. Their past is filled with multiple failed attempts, constant trials and suffering. Their strong commitment towards their goal has made them conquer the peak. A winner is not the one who never fails, but the one who never quits," said Abhinav as he ended his narration.

Abhinav's past journey inspired Rohan. He had a new hope in his eyes. After finishing their breakfast, Abhinav gave the keychain of his first cycle as a farewell gift to Rohan, thinking that it would always remind him of his failed attempts. As they departed, Rohan clicked a few pictures with Abhinav Shukla to post on his Facebook timeline and left with a positive and happy feeling.

The sports day arrived. Rohan entered the school ground with his cycle and a shining smile on his face. He was not scared that he might fail; he was excited to compete and passionate to win. The sports official gave the command, "On your mark, get set, go!"

Later that day, Rohan posted his picture on Facebook where he was standing in the first position on the podium holding his trophy after winning the race. Within a few minutes, the first like on the post came from Abhinav Shukla along with the comment, 'Congrats, champ. Welcome to the world of winning'.

Character cannot be developed in comfort. Only after multiple failures and suffering does one gain the strength, confidence and experience to win. You live life only once, so give it your absolute best. Don't let the fear of failure stop you from doing what you want. The finest iron is obtained only after it is passed through the hottest furnace.

Circle of Life

A good person is hard to find these days. While being kind, helpful and honest is not a challenging task, very few people firmly believe in living a life full of positivity and moral values. Even in the worst situations of life, they don't give up on their principles. One such person is auto rickshaw driver Ganesh Patil. In a profession where cheating people is a very common practice, Ganesh has always been honest and helpful to all his passengers. He never did any kind of tampering with the meter device, never took advantage of an outstation passenger, never overcharged anyone and never said "no" to any person who was desperately in need of a ride.

On a late Monday night, Ganesh was returning home after a hectic day filled with pickups and drops when he was stopped by a person looking for a ride.

"I need to reach this place urgently. Can you please drop me here?" he said as he showed Ganesh a card with the address mentioned on it.

"Yes, I will drop you at this place. Come, get in," replied Ganesh.

“Thank you so much. There were many auto rickshaw drivers whom I had requested before you, but all of them denied me a ride. Finally, you agreed. Thanks a lot,” he said.

“It’s all right, sir. Sometimes passengers have to wait for a while to find a ride that can take them to their desired destination. I am always happy to help those in need,” replied Ganesh.

As they reached the drop point, the passenger gave Ganesh his fare and told him to keep the change and within a fraction of a second, he disappeared. Ganesh finally reached his home and as he was parking his auto rickshaw, he noticed a black leather bag inside it. He immediately recognised it. The bag belonged to his last passenger. Ganesh opened the bag and what he saw was unbelievable.

The bag contained a huge amount of money. Lakhs of rupees in cash. Ganesh quickly closed the bag and took it with him to his home. He did not discuss anything about it with his wife and son. That whole night, Ganesh kept thinking about the money. He believed he had hit the jackpot of his life. With the money inside the bag, he could fulfil all the wishes for himself and his family. All of a sudden, he realised that the money did not belong to him. It was someone’s hard earned money and that person must be having his own requirements for which he needed this money. He could not break his policy of honesty. Ganesh decided to return the money.

The next morning, Ganesh gave a call to the owner of the bag using the contact details mentioned on the bag label. They decided to meet at the same place where Ganesh had dropped him the previous night. Upon reaching the location, Ganesh returned the bag to him. The bag owner thanked Ganesh for his act of honesty and offered him a reward, which Ganesh politely declined.

A month later, the 12-year-old son of Ganesh was admitted to the hospital because of prolonged sickness. Upon studying his entire case, the doctor informed Ganesh that his son had developed an infection. He needed to undergo an operation, for which Ganesh would have to deposit money in advance. The operation had to be conducted within the next 3 days or else there could be a very negative impact on the health of his son as the infection would spread inside his body. Ganesh assured the doctor that he would make arrangements for the money as quickly as possible.

Ganesh did a total sum-up of his savings, fixed deposits, physical assets and the money that could be obtained by selling his wife's jewellery. After combining everything, the money was not sufficient. He tried to borrow money from his family members and relatives, but all of them declined. Even his fellow auto rickshaw drivers did not come forward to help him and some of them also criticised his policy of being kind and honest resulting in his poor financial condition. Ganesh decided to approach banks for a loan, but they rejected his application. Medical NGOs were ready to help, but they could not provide him with money within the next 3 days as they had a time consuming process to follow.

Finally, the day of the operation arrived. Helpless and tense, Ganesh approached the doctor and informed him that he was not able to arrange the money required for his son's operation. The doctor told him not to worry and just sign the papers so that he could proceed with the operation. After completing the required formalities, the operation was done as planned. The entire operation took around 1 hour. As the doctor stepped out of the operation theatre, he informed Ganesh that the operation was successful and his son was out of danger. Ganesh thanked the doctor for his help.

“Thank you, doctor. Thank you so much for your help in such tough times. Today, my son is in a positive condition because of you. But what about the money required for the operation?” questioned Ganesh.

“I have waived all the medical expenses for your son’s treatment, Ganesh. There is no need for you to pay anything to me,” replied the doctor.

“But why, doctor? Any reason behind this sudden change?” Ganesh questioned out of curiosity.

“Ganesh, I hope you remember your passenger to whom you had returned the bag full of money. That very same passenger of yours is a chief trustee of this hospital. When you admitted your son to our hospital, he noticed you as he was also present here that day. After you left to make arrangements for money, he approached me and enquired about your son's case. I told him your situation and he requested that I waive all the medical expenses required for your son’s treatment.

He told me how you gave him a ride when everyone refused him and about your act of honesty when you returned his bag full of money to him. That very same money, which you returned, was used to purchase new medical devices for this hospital. Today, those very same medical devices were used during your son’s successful operation. This is your karma. The result of good deeds done by you in the past. What goes around comes around. This is how the circle of life goes on,” explained the doctor.

For the first time in his life, Ganesh Patil felt that he was rewarded for being a good person. This entire incident made a strong impact on his mind and reassured his faith in his own moral values. Ganesh continued his journey of being kind, honest and helpful, spreading happiness in the lives of others.

Karma is the circle of life, which remains constant. What you give to the world comes back to you. Your present actions will define future reactions in your life. Speak good words, have good thoughts and do good deeds. Be a good person. Keep your circle of life positive.

About the Author

Nirav Parikh is a digital media professional who has spent more than a decade of his career creating powerful and engaging content for a wide range of digital channels. He firmly believes that content is the king and internet is the most effective way to share information and exchange ideas overcoming barriers like time and distance. Apart from writing, Nirav has a keen interest in reading, travelling and adventure sports. Winners is his debut novel which marks his entry in the fiction world.

You can connect with him at
niravparikh@rocketmail.com